# SWIMMING WITH THE SEA MONSTER

## Other books in the series:

Attack of the
LIZARD KING

Charge of the
THREE-HORNED MONSTER

March of the
ARMOURED BEASTS

Flight of the
WINGED SERPENT

Catching the
SPEEDY THIEF

Stampede of the
GIANT REPTILES

Rescuing the
PLATED LIZARD

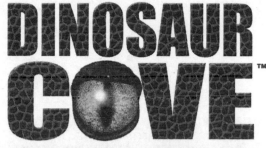

# DINOSAUR COVE™

## SWIMMING WITH THE SEA MONSTER

by
REX STONE

illustrated by
MIKE SPOOR

Series created by
Working Partners Ltd

**OXFORD**
UNIVERSITY PRESS

Special thanks to Jan Burchett and Sara Vogler

To my good friend, Roman Novotny - R.S.

To Christopher - M.S

## OXFORD
### UNIVERSITY PRESS

Great Clarendon Street, Oxford OX2 6DP
Oxford University Press is a department of the University of Oxford.
It furthers the University's objective of excellence in research, scholarship,
and education by publishing worldwide in

Oxford   New York

Auckland   Cape Town   Dar es Salaam   Hong Kong   Karachi
Kuala Lumpur   Madrid   Melbourne   Mexico City   Nairobi
New Delhi   Shanghai   Taipei   Toronto

With offices in

Argentina   Austria   Brazil   Chile   Czech Republic   France   Greece
Guatemala   Hungary   Italy   Japan   Poland   Portugal   Singapore
South Korea   Switzerland   Thailand   Turkey   Ukraine   Vietnam

Oxford is a registered trade mark of Oxford University Press
in the UK and in certain other countries

© Working Partners Limited 2008
Illustrations © Mike Spoor 2008
Eye logo © Dominic Harman 2008

Series created by Working Partners Ltd

The moral rights of the author have been asserted

Database right Oxford University Press (maker)

First published 2008

All rights reserved. No part of this publication may be reproduced,
stored in a retrieval system, or transmitted, in any form or by any means,
without the prior permission in writing of Oxford University Press,
or as expressly permitted by law, or under terms agreed with the appropriate
reprographics rights organization. Enquiries concerning reproduction
outside the scope of the above should be sent to the Rights Department,
Oxford University Press, at the address above

You must not circulate this book in any other binding or cover
and you must impose this same condition on any acquirer

British Library Cataloguing in Publication Data

Data available

ISBN: 978-0-19-272837-1

1 3 5 7 9 10 8 6 4 2

Printed in Great Britain by CPI Cox & Wyman, Reading, RG1 8EX
Paper used in the production of this book is a natural,
recyclable product made from wood grown in sustainable forests.
The manufacturing process conforms to the environmental
regulations of the country of origin.

# FACT FILE

▷ JAMIE AND HIS BEST FRIEND, TOM, HAVE DISCOVERED A SECRET CAVE WITH FOSSILIZED DINOSAUR FOOTPRINTS AND, WHEN THEY PLACE THEIR FEET OVER EACH OF THE FOSSILS IN TURN, THEY ARE MAGICALLY TRANSPORTED TO A WORLD WITH REAL, LIVE DINOSAURS. THE JURASSIC PERIOD WAS KNOWN FOR HAVING LOTS OF SEA LIFE AND THE BOYS WANT TO SEE IT UP CLOSE.
BUT NOT TOO CLOSE...

## JAMIE

- **FULL NAME:** JAMIE MORGAN
- **AGE:** 8 YEARS
- **SIZE:** 1 JATOM*
- **TOP SPEED:** 10 KPH
- **LIKES:** FOSSIL HUNTING AND LEARNING ABOUT DINOSAURS
- **DISLIKES:** BEING STUCK INDOORS

Jamie's eye

Jamie's foot

Jamie's hand

*NOTE: A JATOM IS THE SIZE OF JAMIE OR TOM: 125 CM TALL AND 27 KG IN WEIGHT

**TOM**

- FULL NAME: THOMAS CLAY
- AGE: 8 YEARS
- SIZE: 1 JATOM*
- TOP SPEED: 10 KPH
- LIKES: TRACKING ANIMALS AND EXPLORING WILDLIFE
- DISLIKES: RAINY DAYS

Tom's eye

Tom's hand

**WANNA**

- FULL NAME: WANNANOSAURUS
- AGE: 65 – 80 MILLION YEARS**
- SIZE: LESS THAN A JATOM*
- TOP SPEED: 50 KPH, ESPECIALLY WHEN BEING CHASED BY A T-REX
- LIKES: STINKY GINGKO FRUIT AND BANGING HIS HEAD ON TREE TRUNKS
- DISLIKES: SCARY DINOSAURS

Wanna's head

Wanna's foot

*NOTE: A JATOM IS THE SIZE OF JAMIE OR TOM: 125 CM TALL AND 27 KG IN WEIGHT
**NOTE: SCIENTISTS CALL THIS PERIOD THE LATE CRETACEOUS

## LIOPLEURODON

Liopleurodon's eye

Liopleurodon's Teeth

Liopleurodon's fin

Liopleurodon's tail

- **FULL NAME:** LIOPLEURODON
- **AGE:** 155 – 160 MILLION YEARS***
- **LENGTH:** OVER 10 JATOMS*
- **WEIGHT:** OVER 370 JATOMS*
- **LIKES:** BEING THE FIERCEST AQUATIC PREDATOR OF ALL TIME; HUNTING TASTY ICHTHYOSAURS
- **DISLIKES:** WHEN FOOD GETS AWAY AND BEING CALLED A DINOSAUR. IT WAS A MARINE REPTILE.

*NOTE: A JATOM IS THE SIZE OF JAMIE OR TOM: 125 CM TALL AND 27 KG IN WEIGHT
***NOTE: SCIENTISTS CALL THIS PERIOD THE JURASSIC

Landslips where clay and fossils are

Muddy beach

DINO CAVE

High Tide beach line

Low Tide beach line

Sea

Smuggler's Point

*Hurry up, Tom!* Jamie Morgan thought as a wave lapped around his ankles, swirling the sand beneath his bare feet.

Jamie was going snorkelling in Dinosaur Cove and his best friend Tom Clay was late. He scanned the empty beach, squinting in the sunshine.

Suddenly, he spotted Tom running across the sand with his snorkel and mask dangling over one arm, a bodyboard in the other, and his binoculars round his neck.

'You can't go bodyboarding today,' Jamie
called. 'The sea's as flat as a frisbee.'

'I'm not going bodyboarding.' Tom
grinned, skidding to a halt. 'In fact I'm not
going in *that* sea at all.'

'Not even snorkelling?' asked Jamie,
disappointed.

Tom shook his head. 'Not here.'

'Round the headland then?' asked Jamie.
Tom had lived in Dinosaur Cove all his life so
he knew the best places.

'No, much further away than that.' Tom's
grin was nearly splitting his face. 'But we can
be there in an instant.'

'You mean . . .' Jamie began.

'The Jurassic ocean!' Tom finished.

Jamie and Tom shared a fantastic secret. They'd found a way to visit a world of living dinosaurs.

'Cool!' exclaimed Jamie. He could already feel bubbles of excitement inside. 'Good thing I never go anywhere without my backpack.'

'You've still got the Jurassic ammonite?' Tom asked, as the boys raced towards the cliff path on Smuggler's Point. On their last visit, the boys had discovered that the ammonite fossil they carried with them determined which time period they visited.

'I've got it,' Jamie replied. 'But why do you have a bodyboard when we're going snorkelling?'

'It's for Wanna,' Tom explained as they neared the rocks that led up to their secret cave. 'He can ride while we swim. It's even got one of his prehistoric friends on it.' He stopped at the top of the cliff and turned the board over. A fearsome-looking reptile with four powerful flippers had its mouth open to show off sharp, scary-looking teeth.

Jamie took his Fossil Finder out of his backpack and keyed in *SEA MONSTERS*. *'LEE-OH-PLUR-AH-DON,'* he read. *'MOST SUCCESSFUL AQUATIC HUNTER IN THE JURASSIC, THE LIOPLEURODON IS A TYPE OF PLESIOSAUR.'* Jamie stuffed the Fossil Finder back into his backpack. 'Looks like a plesiosaur wouldn't call Wanna his friend. It would call him dinner.'

The boys scrambled up the rocks to the old smugglers' cave and the hidden entrance to Dino World. They squeezed into the secret chamber at the back, and Jamie shone his torch on to the line of fossilized footprints.

'Ready for action?' said Jamie.

'You bet!' Tom replied.

They put their feet into each clover-shaped print. 'One,
two,
three,
four . . .
five!'

In an instant, Jamie and Tom were walking out among the huge trees of the Jurassic jungle. Giant dragonflies buzzed around them like model aeroplanes in the steaming air.

'Phew! It's as hot as ever,' said Tom, wiping his forehead. 'Just right for a swim.'

*Grunk!*

There was a rustling in the spiky horsetail plants nearby and a little green and brown wannanosaurus burst out.

'Hello, Wanna!' Tom patted their dinosaur friend on his hard domed head and Wanna wagged his tail in excitement.

16

Jamie picked some gingkoes from an overhanging tree. 'Good job his favourite fruit grow in Cretaceous *and* Jurassic times.' He tossed two to Wanna and hid the rest in his backpack. Wanna gobbled up the smelly snacks and rushed about on his stumpy legs, giving the boys sticky licks.

Jamie took out his notebook with the new map of the Jurassic Dino World. 'This says that the sea is south-west from the cave. Got your compass?'

'Course.' Tom pulled it out and pointed to the south-west. 'Through the trees here.'

The three friends set off over the hills,
walking through the conifers and deep ferns
until they arrived on the edge of a cliff,
looking out over the beautiful ocean. To their
right was a calm, sparkling bay shielded from
the waves by a line of jet–black rocks poking
up out of the water.

'Awesome!' exclaimed Tom. 'With those rocks
as barriers, that bay's just like a swimming pool.'

'The perfect place for snorkelling,' said
Jamie. 'And we can climb down that
pathway where the cliff's crumbled away.'

'Last one to the beach is a sea slug!'
yelled Tom.

CHAPTER 2

'Beat you!' Jamie laughed as he clambered over the last of the slippery black slate rocks onto the sand.

'Only just,' said Tom, sliding down beside him. 'Anyway, Wanna's the sea slug.'

Wanna scampered happily up behind.

'Do you think he remembers our last trip to the seaside?' asked Jamie. 'He had quite an adventure with his flying reptile friends.'

Tom grinned. 'Who knows what goes on inside that domed head?'

As the boys headed along the sand, Tom pointed to the biggest rock out in the bay. 'That rock looks like the back of a sea monster with a fin sticking up in the middle.'

'We'll call it Fin Rock,' Jamie decided. The tall rock stood like a gate to the open sea and waves splashed up against it on the ocean side. Beyond the line of rocks, Jamie could see something leaping out of the ocean. 'Wow!'

Tom saw it too and looked through his binoculars. 'There's more than one!' He thrust the binoculars at Jamie.

Jamie knew what they were right away.

'They're ichthyosaurs.'
He flipped open his Fossil
Finder and punched the
keys. The image of a
pointy-nosed prehistoric
dolphin flashed up.
'*ICK-THEE-OH-SOR,*' he read.
'*ATE FISH AND SQUID. EXTINCT
BY THE CRETACEOUS AGE.*'

'They look like they're having fun,' Tom
said. 'We should, too. Let's go snorkelling!'

They dumped the backpack, Tom's
binoculars, and their T-shirts and shoes on a
dry rock, grabbed their masks and snorkels
and waded into the warm shallows. Tom
carried the bodyboard.

The water was so clear that Jamie could
see his toes and the pebbles on the sand.

Wanna dashed after them, but skidded
to a halt at the sight of the tiny waves.

'You wombat!' Tom laughed. 'They won't
hurt you.'

'I know what'll get him in.' Jamie ran back
onto the beach to his backpack and pulled
out a gingko fruit.

He backed slowly into the water keeping it
just out of Wanna's reach. The little dinosaur
followed eagerly, but when the water lapped
over his feet, he darted away again.

Jamie pretended to take a big bite out of
the stinky gingko. 'Yum, yum!'

Wanna licked his lips then took a few steps forwards, wading up to his knees in the water.

'That's it, boy,' Jamie said. 'Come and get your tasty snack.' He put the gingko on the bodyboard as Tom held it still.

*Grunk!*

Wanna scrambled on to the bodyboard making it wobble in the water. Jamie held Wanna's waist as the little dinosaur got his balance.

'He looks like a surfer now,' chuckled Tom, letting go of the board.

'Champion of the waves,' said Jamie.

But when Wanna bent down to eat his gingko, he overbalanced and somersaulted into the sea. He sat in the shallow water looking very surprised.

'Poor old Wanna,' said Jamie, trying not to laugh. The boys helped him on again. This time Wanna managed to stay afloat, but looked mournfully at the gingko which

was floating away.
Jamie grabbed it and
Wanna ate it gratefully.

'I reckon you've
earned that,' said Tom.

Jamie put his hand
firmly through the loop
of the bodyboard's rope.
'Stay still and I'll pull you
along,' he said to Wanna.

'Masks on!' declared Tom.

The boys pulled their
masks over their faces.

'Check!' said Jamie.
'Snorkels in.'

Tom placed the snorkel in his mouth and gave an excited thumbs up.

The boys waded out until the water came up to their armpits and then started swimming, putting their faces in the water so that their snorkels pointed up into the air. Jamie looked down, breathing through his snorkel. Below him, small plants waved in the gentle current and weird, colourful sea creatures darted up and down. An electric-blue sea slug crept over a rock. Then a group of squid-like creatures came swimming by. Their spiral shells were wonderful colours: blues, greens, and purples.

*Real live ammonites!* Jamie thought. *They're so bright.* The ammonites were nothing like

28

the brown and grey fossils he and Tom often
dug up back at Dinosaur Cove.

He could see Tom was having fun too.
He made an O shape with his thumb and
forefinger, the OK sign for divers. Tom signed
back and made a face like a blubbery fish.
Jamie burst out laughing and they both
came up, gasping for air.

Wanna grunked cheerfully at them.
He was obviously enjoying himself
as much as they were.

The boys looked down
again. A shoal of large
cuttlefish drifted past.

They seemed to change colour as they swam, from yellow to orange to blue. Jamie watched fascinated as their eight arms and two long tentacles explored the sand below them. Tom dived below the water, pretending to film them as if he was making a documentary, until they disappeared into some fronds of sea kelp. But Tom wasn't paying attention to where he was swimming and one of his legs became tangled in the underwater leaves.

As quick as he could, Jamie dived down into the tangle to pull his friend free.

'Thanks, Jamie,' Tom said as they surfaced.

'That would have made a good TV programme,' Jamie joked, adjusting his mask on his face. 'Attack of the Killer Kelp!'

Tom laughed, but stopped suddenly. 'Wait—where's the bodyboard?'

Jamie glanced down at his wrist. The rope was gone! 'It must have slipped off.' The boys looked round frantically for their little dino friend.

'Over there,' said Tom, pointing.

Wanna was sitting happily on his board, peering down into the water, completely unaware that he was drifting towards the deep, dangerous ocean beyond Fin Rock.

'Wanna!' yelled Jamie in alarm. The boys swam quickly through the water after their friend, breathing through their snorkels so that they could swim as fast as possible. Jamie could see the seabed sloping away beneath him and the water getting deeper and deeper.

He pulled hard with his arms and kicked furiously. Glancing up through his splashes, he could see that they were nearing the wide gap in the rock barrier, and the rough, foaming water beyond. Wanna was going to be swept out to sea! Jamie couldn't let that happen.

Suddenly, Jamie was close enough to see the bright yellow rope ahead of him. He tried to grab it but it slipped through his fingers. Wanna and the bodyboard had reached the gap next to Fin Rock and were bobbing on the choppy water at the edge of the shallow bay. Beyond was the ocean, so deep and dark that Jamie couldn't see the bottom.

He kicked forwards again and grabbed the loop of the rope, holding on with all his strength as the board tugged against him in the rough water.

'Got him!' he yelled to Tom, his snorkel banging against his cheek.

'Just in time,' Tom said as he swam up.
'Let's get away from here.'

Jamie could feel the board wobbling
violently in the waves. Wanna gave a
frightened grunk.

'Don't worry, boy,' Jamie told him.
'You'll soon be safe.'

But the little dinosaur didn't seem to
understand. He kicked his feet and waved
his tail wildly, eyes wide with fear.

'No, Wanna!' shouted Tom.
'Stop!'

The board rocked
more and more
violently until . . .
SPLASH!
Wanna
disappeared
under the
water.

CHAPTER 3

Jamie dropped the rope, took a deep breath
and dived. He caught hold of Wanna's flailing
front leg and kicked for the surface. Wanna
emerged spluttering, then went under again.
Jamie had taken life-guarding classes, but they
hadn't gone over how to life-save a dinosaur!
He swam round behind Wanna, avoiding the
flapping feet, and grasped him around his
neck, pulling him to the surface. Jamie had
to kick hard to stay afloat as Wanna struggled
in panic.

'Keep still, boy!' he spluttered, as he swam to the edge of Fin Rock. When Jamie finally reached the rock, Tom helped give Wanna a shove to get the little dinosaur up on to the flat part of Fin Rock. Jamie stayed in the water, clinging to the rock, to get his breath back.

Safely on the rock, Wanna sneezed and then spotted some seaweed.

*Grunk!*

He started eating the slimy leaves as if nothing had happened. Jamie smiled and hauled himself out. He pulled his mask down around his neck, like Tom had done.

'Looks like we've lost the bodyboard,' Tom said, indicating out to sea where the board floated away with the waves. 'And if scientists discover a bodyboard next to a dinosaur fossil, we could mess up all of history. Not to mention that we're going to have a hard time getting Wanna back to the beach.'

Jamie groaned. 'I'm sorry. It's all my fault. I dropped the rope.'

'You were saving me from killer kelp at the time.' Tom grinned. 'Anyway, it was my stupid idea to bring Wanna snorkelling.'

Jamie watched the bodyboard being tossed about by the rough sea as he tried to think of how to get Wanna back to shore, when suddenly, a sleek, blue-grey creature jumped over the board, diving smoothly back beneath the surface.

'An ichthyosaur,' breathed Tom. 'Awesome!'

'It's two ickies,' Jamie said as another ichthyosaur batted the bodyboard with its nose, flicking it up into the air like a sea lion with a beach ball.

'Three!' yelled Tom in excitement as one more head popped up in the choppy sea. It caught the board between its teeth and swam away, its friends following behind.

'They're playing with it!' Jamie said.

'I think they're bringing it back,' said Tom.

The ichthyosaurs swam right up to Fin Rock. One of them nudged the bodyboard towards the boys.

*click!*

CLICK, CLICK!

Tom and Jamie bent down to get a close look at the sleek marine reptile eyeing them from the water.

'It's smaller than the other two,' said Jamie. 'I reckon it's a young one, but it's still as big as a dolphin.'

'It has a dolphin's snout,' agreed Tom. 'Only longer and thinner. And an extra set of flippers.'

'And plenty of teeth,' Jamie replied, 'but it seems friendly. Look at that cheeky grin on its face. And those huge eyes.'

CLICK, CLICK, CLICK!

The icky gave the bodyboard another
nudge so that it banged against the rock.

'Thanks!' Tom laughed. 'We'll be more
careful next time.' He fished the board out of
the water.

*Grunk!* Wanna agreed.

The icky waved its flippers and then it
chirped loudly, diving forwards in a perfect
arc and speeding into the shallow water of the
bay. Its friends plunged after it.

'I think they're playing tag,' Jamie said.

Tom slid the bodyboard down onto the
calm water on the bay side of the rock.

'Better get Wanna
back to dry land.'

Jamie put his mask
on, his snorkel back in
and then jumped into
the sea. 'Come on,
boy,' he coaxed,
patting the board.

*Grunk!* Wanna
sounded anxious.

He began to stamp his feet.

'You'll be all right,
I promise,' said Tom. 'We'll
keep the board steady.'

*Grunk,
grunk,
grunk!*

Wanna was jumping up and down now, drumming his tail on the rock. His eyes were fixed on the ocean.

'What's wrong?' asked Jamie.

'He's frightened,' said Tom. 'And so are the ickies.' In the bay the ichthyosaurs were now circling anxiously, making an urgent, clamouring whistle.

Jamie pulled his mask on and ducked under the surface.

From the depths of the ocean, a huge, dark shape was swimming up through the water, heading for the bay. It had a long, crocodile-like head and four strong flippers on its massive body. It was the real-life monster on the bodyboard—a plesiosaur, the deadliest creature in the ocean.

And it was coming straight for him!

# CHAPTER 4

'Plesiosaur,' spluttered Jamie. 'Got to get out!'

Tom didn't waste a second. He hauled his friend on to the rock and pulled the board up after him.

'Thanks,' panted Jamie, pulling down his mask. 'That sea monster's huge.' They turned to see the plessy break the surface of the water. It was at least five times as long as one of the ickies. Its massive jaws stretched like a grin, showing razor–sharp teeth that glistened in the sun.

The boys watched in horror as the plessy swam straight past Fin Rock and into the bay.

'It's after the ickies,' said Tom.

The ickies waited in the bay, watching the plessy approach. Suddenly, with a flick of their tails, they shot towards the gap in the rocks trying to escape into the deep ocean. But the plessy was too big for the ickies to get around.

'They're trapped!' said Jamie.

The plessy kept its enormous body blocking their escape route to the ocean, and each time the ickies tried to make for the open sea, the monster snapped with its fearsome teeth. The water churned like a whirlpool as the creatures struggled.

'The little one's getting tired,' said Tom.

'And that nasty plessy knows it,' added Jamie grimly.

The little icky made another dash for it, but the sea monster plunged down under the water with a huge splash. Jamie and Tom held their breath. When the plessy's head rose again they could see the young ichthyosaur thrashing helplessly in its jaws. Its friends called to it anxiously.

'Oh no!' Jamie felt horrible watching the frantic icky.

The plessy shook its prize in triumph. But one of the ickies dived and swam at the monster, head-butting it hard on the soft underside of its belly. As it turned on its attacker, the second icky rammed it from the other side, making the plessy let go of its prey, which darted off to its friends.

'One—nil to the ickies!' yelled Tom, almost falling off the rock in delight.

'They haven't won yet,' Jamie reminded him. 'They're still trapped.'

'They helped us,' said Tom determinedly.
'We have to help them.'

'You're right,' agreed Jamie. 'But how?'

Tom quickly scanned their craggy island
and went over to a spur of rock with a deep
crack in it. He slid his fingers in and heaved.

'This is no time for weightlifting,' said
Jamie.

'I'm not weightlifting,' puffed Tom, red in
the face with the effort. 'This rock is loose.
We can . . . throw it . . . at the plessy. Might
scare it off.'

Jamie helped. Soon the rock came away.
The boys picked it up between them and
staggered to the water's edge.

'We'll give that creature something to think about!' shouted Tom. '*One, two, three, HEAVE!*'

They lobbed the rock as hard as they could. It fell with a great splash near the monster. But the plessy scarcely flinched.

It ploughed on through the water after its prey. Its thick tail slapped down, splashing another huge wave over Fin Rock. The boys clung on to the fin-shaped rock, digging fingers and toes into any hold they could find. Wanna clung to the boys and grunked anxiously.

'That was close,' gasped Tom.

'Quick!' yelled Jamie. 'The bodyboard.'

The board was floating away into the bay. Tom grabbed the bodyboard's rope just in time.

'Good save,' said Jamie.

Tom was just putting the loop round his wrist to make it secure when Jamie noticed that they were in trouble. 'Uh oh!' Jamie shouted. 'The monster's seen it.'

'Wait,' Tom said. 'I've got an idea.'

Jamie saw the plessy's beady eyes above the surface of the water. They were fixed on the bobbing board. 'That monster will break it to pieces,' Jamie said.

'Hang on,' Tom replied. He gave the rope a shake, making the bodyboard shudder. The plessy glided towards it like a deadly crocodile after its prey, its jaws opening wide. Suddenly it lunged, but Tom quickly flicked the board up and onto the rock and the plessy missed entirely.

'It's just like trout fishing,' he shouted. 'Though I hope I don't catch that monster!'

Jamie gave a whoop of delight. 'Go, Tom!' he called. 'The plessy's forgotten all about the ickies.'

Tom threw the board out again. Again the plessy lunged and Tom jerked it away.

Jamie looked at the ickies progress and saw that they had made it to the gap in the rocks. 'The ickies are escaping!' Jamie cried, but then Tom slipped on the wet rock. He couldn't throw the board out again.

'You do it!' Tom said, throwing the rope up to Jamie.

Jamie grabbed the rope, knowing he needed to keep the monster busy until the ichthyosaurs were safely away. He flung the bodyboard out like Tom had done—but this time the plessy was ready. As soon as it saw the bright board slapping down onto the

water it grabbed it in
its teeth and pulled
hard. Jamie didn't
have a chance to let
go of the rope.

He was catapulted
off the rock and into
the water!

Splash!

# CHAPTER 5

The water roared in Jamie's ears as he was
dragged along the surface by the sea monster
into the bay. White foam swirled around him,
and he wished he had had his mask on.
Everything was blurry, but he could still
see through the water. Suddenly the pulling
stopped. Jamie looked ahead and could just
make out through the water that the
plesiosaur had turned. It floated on the
water, its beady eyes just above the surface.
They were looking straight at him.

It let go of the bodyboard.

*Oh no*, thought Jamie. *I'm dinner!*

As the huge grey body slipped under the surface of the water, coming towards him, Jamie swam frantically for the rock.

He could just hear Tom shouting, 'Hurry, Jamie!'

Jamie knew he couldn't out-swim the plessy, but then he remembered something Tom had told him about predators losing interest when their prey stopped moving. He had nothing to lose. Jamie took a huge

breath and stopped swimming. He quickly
made a star with his arms and legs and lay
there, floating face down in the water.

He watched, his heart pounding hard,
as the plessy swam in a circle below,
watching him.

Jamie knew he mustn't move a muscle.
The bodyboard rope was still tied round his
wrist, tugging at him. He had to fight to keep
his arm still, but his plan was working!

The sea monster wasn't attacking any more. It had lost interest. But Jamie knew that as soon as he lifted his head for air it could be back on to him like a shot.

*Please go!* he thought, desperately willing the sea monster to swim away. But it didn't. Jamie felt as if his lungs were going to burst.

Suddenly he heard a great barrage of squeaking, clicking, and whistling in the water. Something was coming from the deep ocean. The plessy had heard it too.

It whipped round to see what it was. Jamie took his chance. He lifted his head and gulped in air.

Then he saw a wonderful sight. A large pod of sleek grey ichthyosaurs was speeding towards the bay. They leapt over the waves, calling to each other—and Jamie could see their three little icky friends leading the charge!

They made straight for the plessy and began to ram it from all sides. It thrashed about trying to ward off the furious attack.

Jamie struck out for the rock and, with Tom's help, scrambled out of the water. Wanna grabbed the bodyboard in his teeth and pulled it on to the rock.

'Go, ickies!' yelled Tom. 'You can beat that monster.'

The plessy reared and plunged, thrashing out angrily to shake off the whirling mass of ickies. But there were too many for it. They battered and rammed from all sides.

The boys and Wanna watched as the beast swished its massive tail, sending a final huge wave breaking over Fin Rock, then fled for the open sea.

Jamie and Tom leapt up and down in delight while Wanna grunked eagerly. The sea monster had been beaten!

# CHAPTER 6

'That was awesome!' breathed Jamie.

'Those ickies saved your life.' Tom
grinned.

Jamie nodded. 'Too right! They fought off
the fiercest creature in the Jurassic ocean!'

'And they look really pleased about it,'
said Tom, pointing.

The pod of ickies was swimming all
around Fin Rock, their sleek bodies arcing
in and out of the waves. Wanna grunked
happily at them.

'Thank you!' Jamie shouted. 'You were great.' He turned to Tom. 'Shame we don't know icky language.'

'Looks like they understood anyway,' replied Tom. The ickies were sending back a chorus of clicks and whistles. 'I think they're saying, "You're welcome".'

'Let's get back to dry land,' said Jamie, putting his mask back on. 'Hop on board, Wanna. The water's safe now.'

*Grunk!* Wanna looked at the bodyboard which was punctured with large plessy teeth holes.

'Don't worry, boy,' Tom assured him. 'It's still seaworthy.'

Jamie slid into the water, pulling the bodyboard behind him. Tom held it steady and Wanna wobbled on board. Holding one side each, the boys kicked off for shore.

'I can hear something behind us,' Tom shouted suddenly.

Jamie spun round, spluttering as his mouth filled with water. Then he burst out laughing. 'We've got an escort.'

It was the three young ickies swimming along behind the boys, clicking and whistling.

Soon Jamie and Tom were close enough to the shore to stand in the waist-deep water.

The smallest icky swam round their legs, gently butting them as if to say goodbye. Then it sped off to its friends and the three of them swam swiftly away, heading for the open sea.

'Thanks again,' called Jamie after them, pulling off his mask entirely.

## Grunk!

Wanna jumped off the bodyboard and splashed the last few steps to the beach.

The boys picked up their things and made their way back to the cave. Jamie pointed to the huge teeth marks in Tom's board. 'How are we going to explain this?'

'We could say it got attacked by a shark?' suggested Tom.

'No one will believe that,' Jamie replied.

'Well, they won't believe what really happened to it.'

Wanna stuck out his tongue and gave the bodyboard a lick. Then he trotted off towards the cave. When they got close, Wanna began to gather leaves and twigs in his teeth.

'He's making himself a nest,' said Tom.

'Let's help,' said Jamie, grabbing a handful of ferns. The boys got to work, gathering sticks and ferns.

Wanna laid a few twigs down, then nudged them here and there, but when Jamie went to put some branches into the structure Wanna grunked loudly.

'I think he's saying they're the wrong way round.' Tom laughed.

Jamie flipped the branches over. 'Is that better?'

*Grunk, grunk!*

Wanna wagged his tail. Soon he was curled up in his Jurassic nest.

'Sleep tight, boy,' said Tom. The boys had seen on their last visit that Wanna knew how

to go back to the
Cretaceous any time he wanted, so
they said goodbye to their faithful friend
and stepped backwards in the footprints.

As the boys emerged into the bright
sunlight of Dinosaur Cove they were
surprised to see a crowd of people gathered
on the shoreline below.

'What's going on?' Tom asked.

'There's Grandad,' said Jamie. 'Let's find out.'

They scrambled down to the beach as fast
as they could.

Everyone was staring and pointing out
to sea. Tom made sure he kept the bodyboard
behind him so no one would notice the
teeth marks.

'I was wondering where you two had got to,'
Grandad called when he spotted them.
'You've been missing all the fun.'

He nodded out towards the bay. As the boys
watched, the enormous body of a sleek grey
creature broke the surface of the sea. A tall
spout of water shot into the air. A moment
later, a gigantic whale leapt out of the waves.
The crowd clapped and cheered.

'Don't see many whales in these parts.'
Grandad beamed.

'Looks like Dinosaur Cove has got its own sea
monster,' Jamie whispered to Tom with a wink.

'But not as scary as the one back in Dino
World,' Tom whispered back.

'I definitely prefer this one,' Jamie said.

75

DINOSAUR WORLD

BOYS' ROUTE

Humungus
Waterfall

Massive Canyon

Thick
Jungle

Plains

Fin Rock

Jurassic
Ocean

Misty Mountains

Gingko Cave

Discovery Hills

# GLOSSARY

**Ammonite (am-on-ite)** – an extinct animal with octopus-like legs and often a spiral-shaped shell that lived in the ocean.

**Cretaceous (cret-ay-shus)** – from about 65 to 150 million years ago, this time period was home to the widest variety of dinosaur and insect life of any period. Birds replaced winged dinosaurs, while in the sea, sharks and rays multiplied.

**Cuttlefish** – a marine mollusc – not a fish, similar to a squid or octopus, with large W-shaped eyes, eight arms and two tentacles. When they are threatened, they squirt an ink-like fluid or change colour to blend in with their surroundings.

**Gingko (gink-oh)** – a tree native to China called a 'living fossil' because fossils of it have been found dating back millions of years, yet they are still around today. Also known as the stink bomb tree because of its smelly apricot-like fruit.

**Ichthyosaur (ick-thee-oh-sor)** – an extinct marine reptile that looked like a dolphin but had long jaws with sharp teeth, a fin on its back, four flippers and tail.

**Jurassic** – from about 150 to 200 million years ago, the Jurassic age was warm and humid, with lush jungle cover and great marine diversity. Large dinosaurs ruled on land, while the first birds took to the air.

**Kelp** – large brown seaweed. Offers shelter for some sea life and food for others.

**Liopleurodon (lee-oh-plur-ah-don)** – one of the biggest and scariest meat-eating marine reptiles in the Jurassic sea with four powerful flippers, large head but a short neck.

**Plesiosaur (plessy-oh-sor)** – a class of large meat-eating sea reptiles with broad body, large flippers and a short tail. The name means 'near lizard'.

**Wannanosaurus (wah-nan-oh-sor-us)** – a dinosaur that only ate plants and used its hard, flat skull to defend itself. Named after the place it was discovered: Wannano in China.

# Watch out!
## I'm coming soon ...

- CAN YOU ROAR LIKE A T-REX?

- ARE YOU AS QUICK AS A VELOCIRAPTOR?

- OR AS STRONG AS A TRICERATOPS?

**If you're dotty about dinosaurs and round the bend about reptiles, you'll love the Dinosaur Cove website**

# www.dinosaurcove.co.uk

COMPETITIONS

DINOSAURS

BOOKS

GAMES

FACT FILES

Jamie, Tom, and Wanna are waiting to meet you in Dinosaur Cove online . . .